ANIMALS OF THE OCEANS

Whales

Judith Hodge

CONTENTS

Introduction **2**
Different Kinds of Whales **4**
Humpback Whales **6**
Blue Whales **8**
Other Rorquals **10**
Right Whales **12**
Gray Whales **14**
Toothed Whales **16**
Sperm Whales **18**
Belugas, Narwhals and
Beaked Whales **20**
The Whale's Body **22**
Whale Senses **24**
Life Cycle **26**
History of Whaling **28**
The Future for Whales **30**
Index **32**

INTRODUCTION

Whales are monarchs among the animals of the oceans. They are some of the most enormous—and most intelligent—animals on earth. The blue whale, for example, is the largest animal that has ever lived. Full grown, it can be nearly one hundred feet long and weigh one hundred and fifty tons.

The first surprising fact about whales is that they are not fishes. They certainly look like fishes, and they do live in the sea. But they are mammals, like humans.

What distinguishes whales from fishes? There are a number of clues. Fishes extract oxygen from the water through gills. Whales come to the surface to take in air, and they breathe using lungs.

Whales are warm-blooded. This means that their body temperature remains relatively constant. Fishes, on the other hand, are cold-blooded. Their body temperature changes according to the temperature of their environment.

Being mammals also means that whales give birth to live young. Most fishes lay eggs and then leave them to hatch on their own. Mother whales feed their calves with milk and look after them for about a year after they are born.

Millions of years ago, whales used to live on land like other mammals. When they took to the sea, their front legs gradually developed into flippers. They still have two tiny hip bones where their back legs once were.

Above: A baby humpback calf saves its energy by swimming in its mother's slip-stream.

Left: Whales have blowholes, which act as nostrils, on top of their heads. The "blow" is water vapor that condenses in the air when the whale is breathing out.

3

DIFFERENT KINDS of WHALES

Scientists classify whales as belonging to a group of mammals known as cetaceans, which are large sea animals. There are at least seventy-five different kinds of cetaceans. They are divided into two main groups: toothed whales, which have teeth, and baleen whales, which don't have teeth.

Baleen whales have a set of plates which filter food out of the water. These plates, known as baleen, hang from the whale's upper jaw.

Baleen is made of keratin, the same type of material that is found in human hair and fingernails. There are three groups of baleen whales: rorquals, which includes some of the largest whales; right whales; and gray whales.

Toothed whales are generally smaller, with the exception of the sperm whale. There are sixty-five different kinds of toothed whales and they vary greatly in size and shape. Those more than thirteen to fifteen feet long are usually known as whales,

Left: Toothed whales and dolphins keep their first set of teeth—their "baby" teeth—all their lives. These teeth are usually all the same size and shape.

4

Left: Baleen fringes overlap to form a hairy mat in which tiny organisms are trapped. Each group of filter-feeding whales has its own technique for scooping water into the mouth and extracting food from it.

while smaller species are known as dolphins and porpoises. Scientists classify dolphins and porpoises as toothed whales because they have the same basic body features, although most people consider them to be quite different.

Another difference between baleen and toothed whales is that baleen whales have two blowholes, while toothed whales have only one.

Below: Two blowholes can be seen next to each other on the head of this baleen whale.

5

HUMPBACK WHALES

Humpbacks belong to the group of baleen whales known as rorquals. All rorquals have long grooves on the throat and chest.

These grooves enable them to expand their mouths to take in huge quantities of water. As a rorqual's giant mouth closes, water is forced out through the baleen filters. Food is trapped on the inside and swallowed. Humpbacks live in all the world's oceans and mainly feed on krill, small shrimp-like creatures. They also eat small fish.

Humpback whales have only a small hump at the back of the head. They are distinguished more readily by their very long flippers, which can be almost as long as a third of their

Left: A humpback whale's tail works like a fingerprint and is used to identify individual whales. No two tails, with their black-and-white markings and scalloped edges, are alike.

bodies. These are used for steering and for "flippering," making loud splashing noises with their flippers on the water, probably to communicate with other humpbacks.

Humpbacks are also famous for another form of communication, their singing. Male humpbacks sing for hours to attract females. Scientists can tell where a whale comes from by its song, as distinctive tunes are sung by different humpback populations.

Below: Humpbacks put on extremely lively displays. Breaching, or leaping out of the water, is probably done to attract female whales or frighten off potential male rivals.

Above: A rorqual feeds by lunging forward to force water into its mouth, making the pleated throat grooves stretch. The whale takes in so much water that it looks like an enormous tadpole.

Above: The blue whale occasionally raises its tail fluke out of the water when it dives. Dives may last for twenty minutes or more, but usually only take up to half this time.

Below: The people standing next to this beached blue whale look small in comparison. Even the largest dinosaur weighed less than a quarter of the weight of an adult blue whale.

BLUE WHALES

There is no mistaking a blue whale. It's not only blue, it's BIG and blue. In fact, blue whales are the largest living creatures on the planet. At one hundred feet long and weighing over two hundred tons, they make the largest living land animal, the elephant, look puny! At birth, a baby blue whale is already as big as a fully-grown elephant.

Blue whales are gentle giants. They are rorquals, so they feed on krill and other tiny creatures that they filter through their baleen plates. Being so large means that they are able

to frighten off predators and they have plenty of body fat, called blubber, to keep them warm. The downside is that they need to find huge amounts of food to maintain their incredible bulk. An adult blue whale can gulp down eight tons of krill a day.

Newborn blue whales feed on their mother's milk until they are six or seven months old—over twenty-five gallons every day! The milk has a very high fat content, so the baby grows quickly. By the time it is weaned it is already fifty feet long.

Above: Tiny shrimp-like krill are the usual food of baleen whales, and the seas around Antarctica contain huge amounts of this food.

Unfortunately, their huge size made blue whales easy targets for hunting. They were protected in the mid-1960s, by which point it is estimated that over a third of a million blue whales had been killed. Whale populations in some oceans may never recover from such intense whaling.

OTHER RORQUALS

Most rorquals, with the exception of the humpback, are long, streamlined animals. They are sometimes called finback whales because they have a dorsal (back) fin.

Rorquals are found in all the oceans of the world. Their diet can vary within a species depending on which hemisphere they live in. For example, fin whales found in the Southern Hemisphere eat krill, while those living north of the equator also eat small fish such as herring.

At thirty feet, minke whales are the smallest of the rorquals. Their smaller size meant that they were not originally targeted by whaling fleets. As larger whale species have been depleted, however, minke whales are now the only whales hunted in large numbers.

Like minke whales, Bryde's (pronounced Broodahs) whales are blue-gray on top with white stomachs. They live only in tropical and subtropical seas and grow much longer than minkes, reaching forty-five feet. Another unusual feature is that they eat mainly small fish and squid.

Above: Minke whales are often found feeding around the edge of the ice shelf in polar seas. They are more inquisitive than many rorquals.

Right: The fin whale's backward sloping dorsal fin distinguishes it from other rorquals and helps identify it at sea. Both the sei and minke whales' fins stand more upright.

Fin and sei whales are the other large rorquals. The two species look similar, with distinctive black top halves and white bellies. Fin whales have a two-tone jaw: the lower jaw is white on the right side and black on the left. Sei whales grow up to fifty-five feet long, whereas fins can reach eighty feet.

Left and below: Bryde's whales are the only rorquals that don't migrate to polar waters and tend to stay in warmer waters all year round. They are also more lively than some other species, often breaching completely out of the water.

11

RIGHT WHALES

Right whales are baleens, but they feed in a different way than rorquals. They don't open their mouths as wide when they trawl for krill. Their huge heads, which make up about a third of their body, contain much larger baleen plates with which to filter food.

From a right whale's upper jaw hang two hundred to two hundred and seventy pairs of baleen plates like giant curtains. These baleen are the longest of any whale species, growing to fifteen feet. The mouth of the right whale has to be very arched, with lips sometimes as high as eighteen feet, to fit the enormous plates of baleen inside.

A large whale without a dorsal fin can only be a right whale. There are four families of right whales—the bowhead; the northern right; the southern right; and the pygmy right—and they are all threatened with extinction.

Left: The right whale is surprisingly agile considering its bulky shape and slow swimming speed. Southern right whales have even been seen doing head stands with their flukes in the air.

The bowhead, which is only found in the Arctic Ocean, and the black right both grow to about sixty feet long, but the black right has smaller baleen. The pygmy is only about twenty feet long and is very rarely seen.

A right whale's body is thick and solid and right whales are slow swimmers, averaging less than four miles per hour. Right whales are often hit by boats because they travel so slowly. Barnacles are even able to hitch a ride on their skin.

Above: A bowhead is distinguished from a right whale by its white chin patch and a lack of callosities or growths on its head. The paddle-like flippers are common to both species.

Left: Callosities or hardened bits of skin form on the right whale's head. The pattern of these is different on each animal and helps to identify individuals.

GRAY WHALES

Just as the humpback whale doesn't have a pronounced hump, the gray whale may be black or dark gray. White patches on its mottled skin are barnacles and lice, which live on these slow-moving whales. Gray whales hold the record for skin parasites, and sick animals are often completely covered with them.

More stocky than most rorquals, gray whales have a series

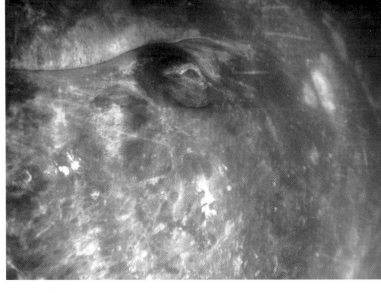

Above: The gray whale's eyes, like those of all whale species, are able to see both underwater and in the air.

Below: Parasites like whale lice have a particular liking for gray whales, feeding on flaking skin and on food scraps that fall from the whale's mouth.

14

of bumps along the ridge of their bodies. Despite similarities with other baleens, the gray whale is unusual enough to be in a group of its own. It is the only cetacean to feed regularly on organisms found in mud on the bottom of shallow seas.

It also has a unique way of finding its food. The gray whale cruises along the ocean floor like a giant vacuum cleaner, sucking up sand and straining out tiny animals with its baleen. It will also eat small fish and tiny organisms called plankton in the surrounding water.

The gray whale migrates between breeding grounds in northern Mexico and feeding grounds in the northern reaches of the Pacific Ocean. A once-thriving population in the Atlantic Ocean was killed off by whalers in the eighteenth century. Gray whales were almost extinct by 1946, but now the California population has recovered in numbers to its original level of about twenty thousand.

Whalers used to call gray whales "devil fish" because they would ram and sink the small boats of the harpooners. However, today females and young grays often come close to small tourist boats in the breeding lagoons and seem to enjoy close contact with people.

Above: The gray whale usually feeds on its side, first moving along the ocean floor stirring up the mud. It then retraces its tracks to filter the cloud of food-filled sand.

TOOTHED WHALES

Each toothed whale has simple, peg-like teeth that are all the same size and last a lifetime. Among the species of toothed whales, however, there is a wide range of numbers, shapes and sizes of teeth. This makes them unusual among carnivores, or flesh-eaters, which usually have different types of teeth for tearing and chewing. By

Above: Short-finned pilot whales are very similar to the long-finned species, but with different shaped and sized flippers. They also have a different number of teeth.

Right: Orca have sharp teeth in both their upper and lower jaws. They catch a greater variety of prey than any other marine mammal.

16

contrast, toothed whales typically swallow their food whole.

Toothed whales less than twelve feet long are usually classified as dolphins. One exception is the family Globicephalidae. It includes two species of pilot whale (long- and short-finned); killer whales; false killer whales; pygmy killer whales; and the melon-headed whale. Although all six species have "whale" in their common names, they are thought to be more closely related to true dolphins than to any of the large whale species.

Killer whales, also known as orca, and pilot whales are the largest of the dolphins. They have no beak, a domed head and fewer teeth than most dolphins. Orca are found in oceans all over the world. They are known as killer whales because of their reputation as highly efficient hunters. Of the six Globicephalidae species, orca is the only one found worldwide. The other species are restricted to the warmer waters of both hemispheres.

Right: Porpoises and dolphins are among the largest groups of toothed whales.

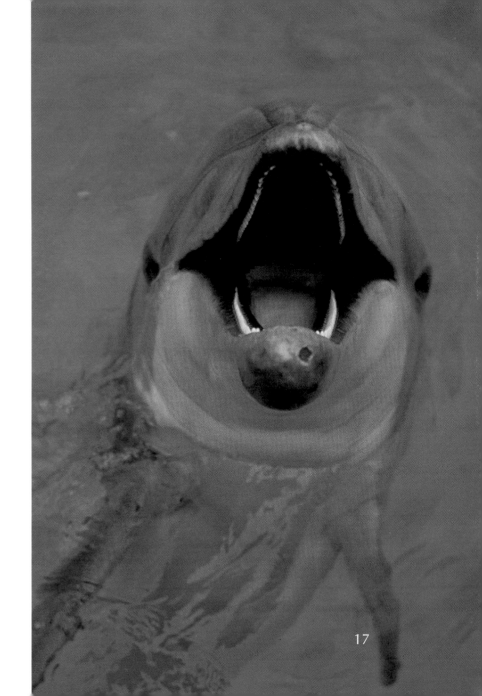

SPERM WHALES

With their huge square heads and massive teeth, sperm whales, also known as cachalots, are by far the largest of the toothed whales. A male may grow up to sixty feet and weigh forty-four tons, while a female reaches forty feet. A sperm whale must look as terrifying a sight to a squid as Moby Dick, the most famous sperm whale of them all, looked to Captain Ahab in the novel by Herman Melville!

Some large squid live at great depths, but sperm whales are able to feed on them. A large sperm whale may eat as much as a ton of squid and cuttlefish a day, and is able to dive deep to find them. Sperm whales can dive as deep as nine thousand seven hundred and fifty feet and hold their breath for up to two hours. Scientists think that the sperm whale's large, square forehead may help it to dive to these amazing depths.

Right: Older sperm whales, particularly males, may have large white patches or scar tissue on their heads from fights with other males or sometimes with giant squid.

Another secret weapon appears to be the sperm whale's own form of a stun gun. They produce powerful sounds or "clangs," which seem to stun prey such as squid, deepwater sharks and barracuda.

Like humpback whales, sperm whales seem to communicate with each other through slow patterns of audible clicks called codas, which they repeat to each other.

They are found in all the oceans, with females and juveniles living in tropical and temperate waters. Two smaller relatives, the dwarf and the pygmy sperm whales, grow to ten feet long and are found only in warmer seas.

Above: Family groups of female sperm whales live together with their calves, and even "babysit" each other's young. Young males normally leave when they become teenagers and join "bachelor" pods.

Right: Squid is a staple food of sperm whales in most areas. However, legendary battles between these whales and giant squid are more myth than reality: most of the squid they catch are medium-sized.

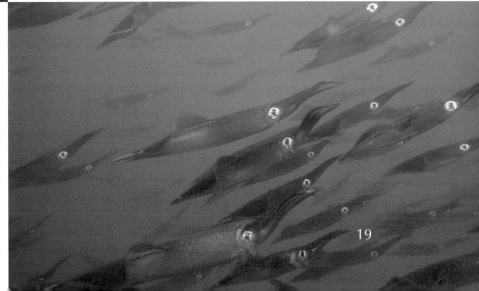

BELUGAS, NARWHALS and BEAKED WHALES

Belugas are very social animals and are called the "canaries of the sea" because of the noises they make, such as whistles and clangs. They grow to ten or fifteen feet and are also known as "white whales," due to their creamy white color when adult. Belugas are mainly found in the Arctic Ocean and live on fish and squid.

Narwhals are grayish on top and white underneath, with dark spots all over the body. There's no mistaking a male narwhal. With their distinctive tusk, they look like unicorns of the deep. Both males and females have only two teeth in their upper jaw, but in the male one of these develops into a long spiral tusk up to ten feet long. Narwhals use them for ritualized fighting.

Below: Narwhals are never far from ice, living mainly in arctic and subarctic waters. Groups are seen in breaks in the ice as it retreats in warmer months.

Beaked whales are found only in the Northern Hemisphere, and not much is known about their mysterious lives. Like sperm whales, they feed in the depths of the ocean on squid and fish. There are eighteen different species, but they are seldom sighted.

Most of the information we have about beaked whales comes from stranded animals found on beaches. From these specimens, people have learned that some beaked whales grow to only fifteen feet, while others reach nearly forty feet, and that they have only two or four teeth in the lower jaw and no upper teeth. This is characteristic of squid-catchers.

Above: Belugas are one of only two species of cetaceans that can change their facial expressions. While this makes them look rather adorable, the real reason for this is probably to help them with feeding.

Left: Male narwhals are often seen "crossing swords" on top of the water in what seems like playful behavior. Their tusks are used much like a deer's antlers for threatening or fighting rival males.

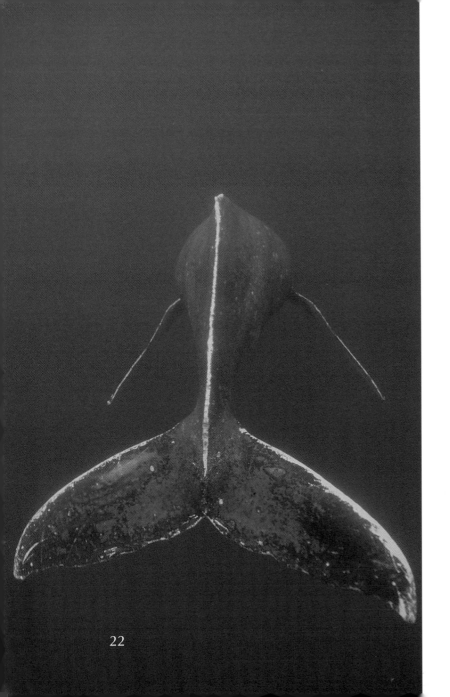

THE WHALE'S BODY

Some parts of the whale's body, such as its rib-cage, backbone, hip bones and shoulder blades, are the same as other mammals that live on land. But many of the animal's special characteristics have developed through living in the sea.

They can only grow so large because their bodies are supported in water. If a large whale becomes stranded on shore, its huge body weight can crush vital organs such as lungs.

In the water, whales need to surface to breathe through nostrils, or blowholes, in the tops of their heads. Powerful muscles close up the blowhole when the animal dives again. Whales can hold their breath for a long time underwater. A sperm whale can stay below for seventy-five minutes before surfacing for another breath.

The whale's powerful tail fluke is another adaptation for life in the ocean. It pushes the

Left: A whale's streamlined body and smooth skin helps it swim easily.

whale forward by moving up and down, unlike a fish's tail, which moves from side to side.

Land mammals have skin covered in hair to keep them warm. Whales only have a few bristles on their heads. Instead, they have a layer of blubber or fat for insulation. Blubber has other uses, too: they can live on it when there's not much food around, and since blubber is lighter than water, it helps them keep afloat.

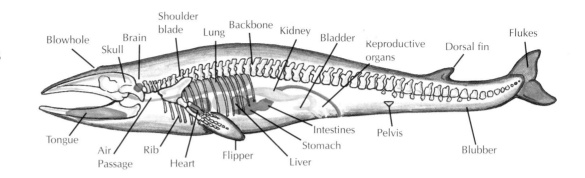

Blowhole   Skull   Brain   Shoulder blade   Lung   Backbone   Kidney   Bladder   Reproductive organs   Dorsal fin   Flukes

Tongue   Air Passage   Rib   Heart   Flipper   Intestines   Stomach   Liver   Pelvis   Blubber

Above: Diagram of a whale's body.

Right: The skeleton of a blue whale, put together from pieces lying near each other on the Antarctic Peninsula, shows the animal's long jaw bone.

23

Above: It is important to keep the upper surface of stranded animals wet with cloths soaked in sea water until rescuers arrive to help refloat the animals.

Below: Orcas often pull their heads out of the water together and hop along the surface. This is called spy-hopping, as the animals are looking out for prey like penguins and seals.

WHALE SENSES

Hearing is as important to whales as eyesight and smell are to the majority of land mammals. Most whales, with the exception of orca, have poor vision and no sense of smell. They have to rely on their sharp hearing to give them information about what's going on around them. Whales can hear a very wide range of sounds, both low- and high-pitched, that are outside the range of human hearing.

In the dark and murky depths of the ocean, good eyesight is often little help in navigating and locating prey. Instead, whales send out sounds which bounce off objects. From these echoes they can tell how far away an object is, as well as its size and other information. This system is known as echolocation.

Mass strandings of whales are not common, and generally only occur with toothed whales. The strong social bonds that hold a group of whales together often cause the whole herd to beach themselves trying to help a sick or distressed whale.

Scientists don't know what causes whales to beach themselves, but they think whales may use the earth's magnetic field to navigate. Stranding often happens where the signals from these magnetic maps are at confusing angles to the land.

Whales also produce noises for other reasons. The most famous of these are the songs of the humpback whale, but others are also thought to use sounds to communicate with whales of the same species. The low rumbling sounds of blue whales can be heard by other whales up to one thousand one hundred miles away.

Above: Male humpback whales sing to attract females, with each individual animal having his own song. This "tune," with different phrases repeated sometimes for hours, develops over the years.

LIFE CYCLE

The life span of whales varies from thirty years for smaller toothed whales to sixty or seventy years for sperm whales. Some baleen whales can live up to eighty years, dying of old age if they are not hunted.

Sharks and orca will prey on young or sick whales, but apart from these exceptions whales have very few natural enemies. Other causes of death result from strandings, to which some species are particularly prone, or being hunted by people or caught accidentally in fishing nets.

Migration plays a very important part in the life cycle of most baleen whales. Every year, pregnant females make the journey from the rich feeding grounds of the Arctic or the Antarctic to give birth in the warmer waters of the breeding grounds. Males also accompany them as this is where mating

Right: The tightest social unit among whales is the mother/calf bond. Young whales are totally dependent on their mothers, with some whales being suckled for two years or more.

26

takes place. Summer is spent feeding and building up large stores of blubber to last through a winter in tropical oceans.

Pregnancy usually takes from ten to twelve months. The mother looks after its offspring and suckles it for up to a year. Young whales are usually large enough to return to the feeding grounds by the end of spring. With the notable exception of sperm whales, most toothed whales don't migrate over long distances except to find fresh food supplies.

The social life of whales varies between species. Blue whales normally feed by themselves or in small groups, because they need all of the food they find for themselves. Other species, such as sperm whales and killer whales, stay in particular family groups for years.

Above: Humpback whales are often seen feeding in groups, sometimes of up to twenty or more animals. This type of cooperative feeding is unusual in baleen whales.

Below: Female sperm whales and their young, like this group, stay in warm waters all year round. Males have to migrate every year to find them.

HISTORY of WHALING

Whales have been hunted since prehistoric times: a four thousand-year-old Norwegian rock drawing shows whaling scenes. At first, whales were hunted near the shore from small boats. Yet even when whalers used hand-held harpoons, too many animals were killed and whalers had to keep finding new hunting grounds. Right whales—they were the "right" ones to catch because they were slow swimmers and floated when dead—were the first to be overhunted.

Many products were made from whales, such as brushes and corsets from baleen and oil for lamps and candles. Ambergris from the intestines of sperm whales was particularly prized as a base for perfumes.

Until 1860, only slow-moving whales could be killed. But the invention of the harpoon gun

Below: This woodcut from the 1850s shows some of the perils of whaling. Whalers set forth in small boats from the main sailing ship, armed only with hand-held harpoons.

28

Above: Minke whales, once thought to be too small for whaling, are still hunted by some countries. The whales mainly end up as food.

whale became more scarce, whalers started hunting smaller ones, such as fin and then sei whales. Between 1900 and 1940 more whales were slaughtered than in the previous four hundred years!

The International Whaling Commission (IWC) was set up in 1946 to regulate the whaling industry, but continued to set quotas that were too high until the 1970s. By 1986 there was a worldwide ban on whaling—there were too few whales left for it to be sustainable.

and steam-powered whaling boats enabled whalers to start hunting the faster-swimming rorquals.

The greatest disaster for whale numbers came in the early 1900s with the factory ships. These enormous boats, equipped with spotter planes and sonar tracking equipment, processed dead whales at sea. As larger species such as the blue

Right: Whalers sometimes passed the time on long voyages carving whales' teeth and bones. These pieces are called scrimshaw. Sperm whales' teeth were especially favored.

29

THE FUTURE for WHALES

Public opinion played an important part in the ban on commercial whaling. Campaigns by conservation groups have done much to turn the tide against whaling in many countries.

However, most of the whale species that were commercially hunted, such as the blue, bowhead, and right whales, are still on the endangered list. The numbers of some species are so low that they may never recover. Blue whales, for example, have been protected for several decades. Some other species, such as beaked whales, have always been very rare.

Despite this, traditional whaling nations such as Japan, Iceland and Norway are calling for commercial whaling to resume, arguing that stocks of smaller whales such as minke are plentiful. Many of them have continued to take whales, with special permits for "scientific research" issued

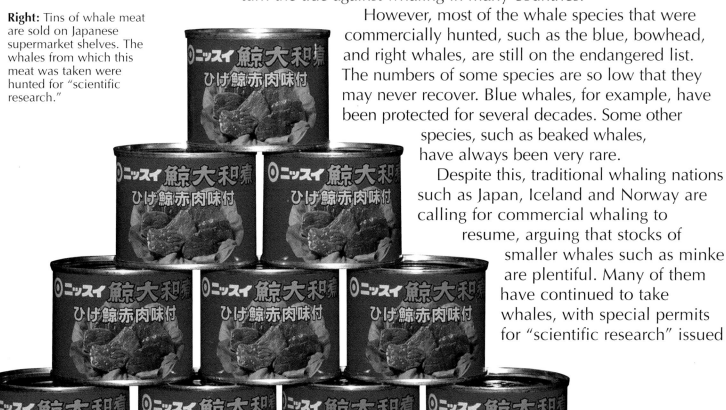

Right: Tins of whale meat are sold on Japanese supermarket shelves. The whales from which this meat was taken were hunted for "scientific research."

since the ban. The IWC also allows some indigenous peoples, such as the Inuit of Alaska, to continue hunting using traditional methods.

Hope for the whale's future could lie in the rise of interest in whale-watching. There are now a number of countries worldwide where tourists can catch a glimpse of whales in their natural habitat.

Above right: Whale-watching is a popular tourist attraction, with hundreds of thousands of people making journeys out to sea each year in the hope of catching sight of a whale.

Right: "Save the whales" has become a universal rallying cry, highlighting not just the plight of whales and other marine mammals, but drawing attention to widespread human abuse of the environment.

31

INDEX

ambergris 28
baleen 4–5, 12
baleen whales 4, 12
beaked whales 21, 30
belugas 20, 21
blowholes 3, 5, 22
blubber 9, 23
blue whale 2, 8–9, 27, 30
body 22–23
bowhead whale 12, 13, 30
breaching 7
Bryde's whale 10, 11
cachalot (see sperm whale)
callosities 13
communication 7, 19, 25
conservation 30–31
diving 22
dolphins and porpoises 5, 17
echolocation 25
fin whale 11
finback whales 10
flippering 7
flippers 6–7
gray whale 4, 14–15
hearing 24
humpback whale 3, 6–7, 25, 27
indigenous peoples 31

International Whaling Commission 29, 31
keratin 4
krill 6, 9
life span 26, 27
migration 26
minke whale 10, 29, 30
Moby Dick 18
narwhals 20, 21
orca (killer whale) 16, 17, 24, 27
pilot whales 17
right whales 4, 12–13, 28, 30
rorquals 4, 6, 7, 10–11
sei whale 11
short-finned pilot whale 16
skeleton 23
social bonds 25, 26, 27
sperm whale 18–19, 27, 28, 29
squid 18, 19
strandings 21, 24, 25
tail (fluke) 1, 8, 22–23
teeth 4, 16
toothed whales 4, 16–17
whale lice 14
whale meat 30
whale-watching 31
whaling 9, 28–29, 30

First published in 1997 by David Bateman Ltd.,
30 Tarndale Grove, Albany Business Park,
Albany, Auckland, New Zealand

Copyright © David Bateman Ltd., 1997

First edition for the United States and Canada
published by Barron's Educational Series, Inc., 1997

Text: Judith Hodge, B.A. (Hons)
Editorial consultant: Michael Donoghue, M.Sc.
Photographs: Malcolm Francis, Key-Light Image Library,
Natural Images, New Zealand Picture Library, Clive Roberts
(Museum of New Zealand), Sea Watch Foundation, Robert
Suisted, Kim Westerskov
Illustrations: Caren Glazer
Design: Errol McLeary

All inquiries should be addressed to:
Barron's Educational Series, Inc.
250 Wireless Boulevard
Hauppauge, New York 11788

Library of Congress Catalog Card No. 97-19630
International Standard Book No. 0-7641-0261-3

Library of Congress Cataloging-in-Publication Data
Hodge, Judith, 1963–
    Whales / Judith Hodge.
        p. cm. — (Animals of the oceans)
    Originally published: Auckland, N.Z. : D. Bateman
        Ltd., 1995.
    Includes index.
    Summary: Describes the physical characteristics,
habits, and natural environment of some of the most
enormous and intelligent mammals on earth.
    ISBN 0-7641-0261-3
    1. Whales—Juvenile literature. 2. Cetacea—
Juvenile literature. [1. Whales.] I. Title. II. Series.
QL737.C4H624 1997
599.5—dc21   97-19630
                                                              CIP
                                                              AC

Printed in China
9 8 7 6 5 4